The Way the Storm Stops

BY **Michelle Meadows**

ILLUSTRATED BY **Rosanne Litzinger**

HENRY HOLT AND COMPANY | NEW YORK

Henry Holt and Company, LLC
Publishers since 1866
115 West 18th Street, New York, New York 10011
www.henryholt.com

Henry Holt is a registered trademark of Henry Holt and Company, LLC
Text copyright © 2003 by Michelle Meadows
Illustrations copyright © 2003 by Rosanne Litzinger
All rights reserved.
Distributed in Canada by H. B. Fenn and Company Ltd.

Library of Congress Cataloging-in-Publication Data
Meadows, Michelle.
The way the storm stops / by Michelle Meadows ; illustrated by Rosanne Litzinger.
Summary: A mother soothes her child to sleep during a thunderstorm.
[1. Mother and child—Fiction. 2. Thunderstorms—Fiction. 3. Stories in rhyme.]
I. Litzinger, Rosanne, ill. II. Title.
PZ8.3.M4625 Way 2003 [E]—dc21 2002004592

ISBN 0-8050-6595-4 / First Edition—2003 / Designed by Donna Mark
Printed in the United States of America on acid-free paper. ∞
1 3 5 7 9 10 8 6 4 2

The artist used watercolor with gouache and colored pencil
on Italian Fabriano fine watercolor paper to create
the illustrations for this book.

For my favorite boys, Richard and Chase

—M. M.

For Emma

—R. L.

Pitter, pitter
Plam, plam
On my windowpane

Hiss, hiss
Tatter, tatter
Falls the pounding rain

Rumble, rumble
Crack, crack
Thunder at our door

Rolling, rolling
Bam, bam
Shakes my bedroom floor

Razz, razz
Flash, flash
Sparks the dazzling light

Scrunch, scrunch
Shiver, shiver
Curl my body tight

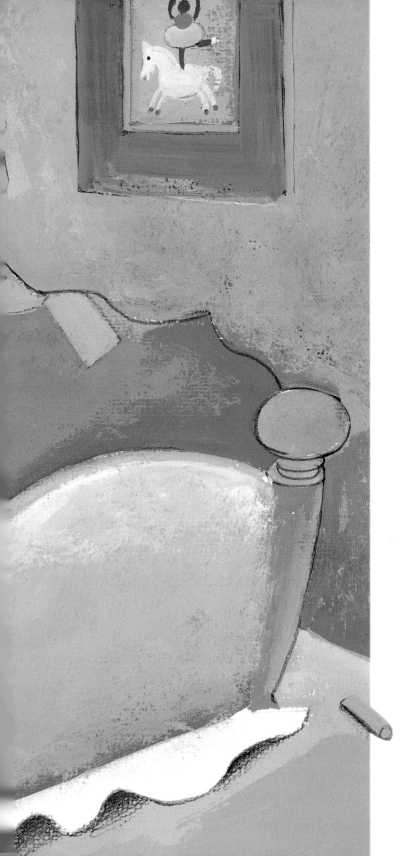

Peep, peep
Blink, blink
Hiding in the dark

Creep, creep
Boom, boom
Thunder makes its mark

Tip, tip
Tap, tap
Mommy's by my side

Scoop, scoop
Rub, rub
Giving me a ride

Squeeze, squeeze
Rock, rock
Floating in her chair

La, la
Hum, hum
Tickled by her hair

Plish, plish
Raf, raf
Softening up the storm

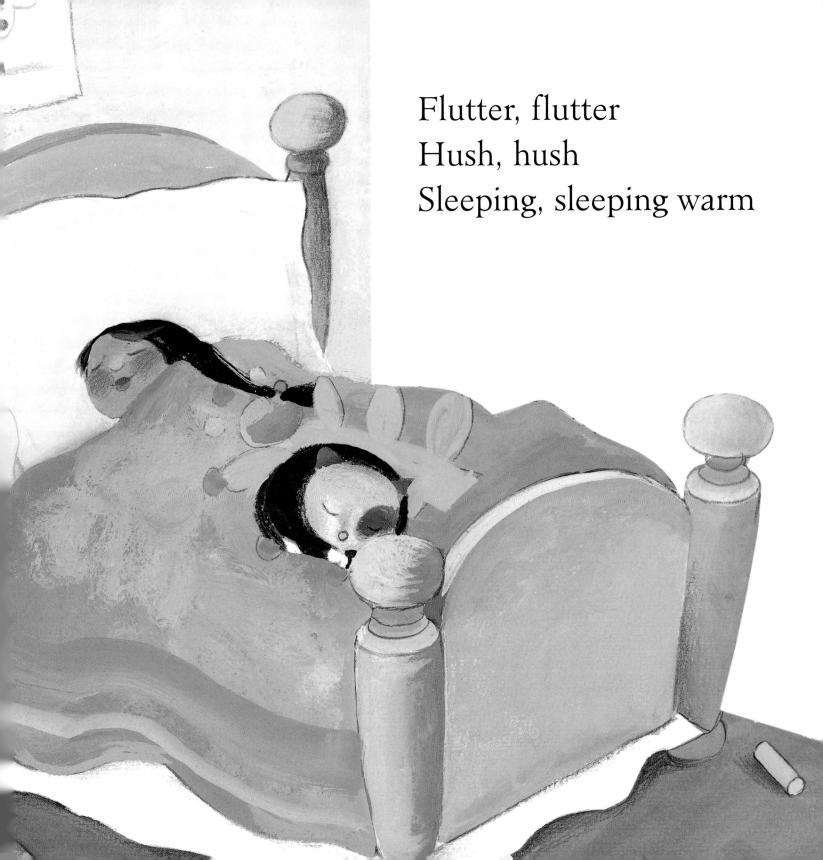

Flutter, flutter
Hush, hush
Sleeping, sleeping warm